WHEN THE WATER CLOSES OVER MY HEAD

OTHER BOOKS BY DONNA JO NAPOLI

The Bravest Thing
Jimmy, the Pickpocket of the Palace
The Magic Circle
The Prince of the Pond
Shark Shock
Soccer Shock

WHEN THE WATER CLOSES OVER MY HEAD

Donna Jo Napoli

illustrated by

NANCY POYDAR

PUFFIN BOOKS

PUFFIN BOOKS
Published by the Penguin Group
Penguin Books USA Inc., 375 Hudson Street, New York, New York 10014, U.S.A.
Penguin Books Ltd, 27 Wrights Lane, London W8 5TZ, England
Penguin Books Australia Ltd, Ringwood, Victoria, Australia
Penguin Books Canada Ltd, 10 Alcorn Avenue, Toronto, Ontario, Canada M4V 3B2
Penguin Books (N.Z.) Ltd, 182-190 Wairau Road, Auckland 10, New Zealand

Penguin Books Ltd, Registered Offices: Harmondsworth, Middlesex, England

First published in the United States of America by Dutton Children's Books,
a division of Penguin Books USA Inc., 1994
Published in Puffin Books, 1996

1 3 5 7 9 10 8 6 4 2

THE LIBRARY OF CONGRESS HAS CATALOGED THE DUTTON EDITION AS FOLLOWS:

Napoli, Donna Jo.
When the water closes over my head/ by Donna Jo Napoli;
illustrated by Nancy Poydar.—1st ed.
p. cm.
Summary: When his family goes on vacation to visit his grandparents in Iowa,
nine-year-old Mikey is continually faced with his fear of drowning.
ISBN 0-525-45083-1
[1. Fear—Fiction. 2. Swimming—Fiction. 3. Family life—Fiction.]
I. Poydar, Nancy, ill. II. Title.
PZ7.N15Wh 1994 [Fic]—dc20 93-14486 CIP AC

Puffin Books ISBN 0-14-037996-7

Printed in the United States of America

To my guys—

Barry and Michael and Nicholas and Robert—

the fearless and peerless foursome,

with love

CONTENTS

WHEN THE WATER CLOSES OVER MY HEAD

1

The Slingshot

Mikey stuffed one more pair of shorts into his backpack. He looked at his green bathing suit, sitting there in the bureau. He didn't like water, and he couldn't swim. No one could make him go in the water this summer. He shut the drawer.

Mikey walked around the house, checking all the doorknobs for rubber bands. He had six in his pocket so far. He needed at least ten for the superdeluxe slingshot he had in mind. He planned to take that slingshot to fourth grade with him at the end of the summer.

Mikey was good at sports. He was fast with his feet and hands. He was always pitcher at baseball because he had great aim. He knew with practice he could be a sharpshooter at the slingshot. But swimming? No way.

"Mikey," his mother called. "Do you know where your brother is? I can't pack his part of the suitcase without him."

"No," Mikey called back as he stuck a fat red rubber band in his pocket. This one was strong. It would shoot far.

"Well, find him for me, please, would you?"

"Ask Victoria," Mikey called in a louder voice. So far that morning he had helped clean out the car for the trip, taken their bird in his cage to the neighbor's house for safekeeping, and finished his own packing. That made three chores already. It was Victoria's turn for chores. After all, she was the big sister.

"I'm asking you," Mamma said. "Now!"

Mikey jammed three more rubber bands into his pocket and went out the back door, shouting, "Calvin, where are you?"

Mikey went to the sandbox first. That was Calvin's favorite spot. The lid was off, and the sandbox toys were scattered across the yard. Mikey automatically picked up the pink rake that Calvin loved and aimed carefully. It landed on top of the plastic jeep in the middle of the sandbox.

He went around to the front of the house. There was a box of crayons dumped on the porch. Some of the crayons had been chewed up. Yippy, their puppy, had been at work.

Mikey was headed for the garage when he saw Calvin. Calvin and Julie were strapped into their car seats in the third row of the station wagon.

"Hey, Calvin. Mamma wants you. What are you doing in the car?" Mikey opened the tailgate. Calvin and Julie smiled at him. Yippy jumped up from between them and licked Mikey's face.

"I'm all strapped in, Mikey, see? I did it myself. And I did Julie, too." Calvin patted his seat belt.

"Well, unstrap yourself. Mamma needs you."

"I'm ready to go, Mikey." Calvin nodded his head as he talked. "I'm all ready to go to Iowa. I'm not going to be left behind. I'm going, too."

"Me too," Julie chimed in. Her fat, round cheeks were red from the heat. Her blond hair clumped in ringlets.

Mikey looked from Julie back to Calvin. Their faces were worried and hopeful. Why had he been born into such a dumb family? "Calvin, you worm brain. Of course you're going to Iowa. We're all going to Grandma and Grandpa's. But we're not leaving till tomorrow. Come out of the car now. Come on. Come out."

"I'll just wait here till tomorrow," said Calvin.

"You'll be afraid when it gets dark."

"I have my sleep blanket." Calvin held up his shabby blue blanket. Julie held up her rag doll. "Julie's not afraid either," said Calvin.

Mikey pulled the rubber bands out of his pocket and counted them. He sighed. "Look, Calvin, you just get out of the car and go upstairs and I'll let you help me make my slingshot."

"You're making a slingshot? Oh, goody!" Calvin put his hands on the seat belt buckle. "I love to help you make slingshots, Mikey. What's a slingshot?"

—

Mikey arranged the rubber bands by size on the dining room table. Then he attached them together, starting with the skinny ones. Next he added two medium bands at one end and one at the other. It wasn't equal, but there was nothing he could do about it. These were all the medium-size bands in the house. Last of all, he attached a fat band at each end. Now he had a superdeluxe slingshot band. It was time to find a superdeluxe forked stick.

Mikey went out the back door. Yippy bounded out from under the bushes and tagged along at his heels. It didn't take long to find the perfect stick. It had just the right spring to it. Mikey imagined himself face-to-face with a robber. The robber would think a boy his size had to be unarmed. But Mikey would whip out his slingshot and zap the guy between the eyes. The robber would take off screaming. Mikey dragged the stick into the dining room with grim determination, letting the door swing shut in Yippy's face.

Calvin sat at the dining room table, humming and working away busily at the rubber bands.

Mikey looked closer. "What are you doing?" He dropped his stick and ran to the table. Calvin had separated the rubber bands into three piles: green, red, and brown. Mikey gasped. "Look what you did to my slingshot!"

Calvin started to cry. Calvin always started to cry. There he'd go and do something awful to Mikey, and when Mikey would get mad at him, he'd cry.

"Mikey." Mamma's voice rose in a half question, half scold. She came downstairs. "Mikey, what's going on?"

"Calvin ruined my slingshot."

"I hate slingshots," said Mamma.

"You hate everything fun."

"You say sorry, Michael Nelson. And you catch hold of yourself right now."

"I'm sorry," Mikey shouted.

"He doesn't mean it, Mamma," said Victoria in a quiet voice. She stood on the stairs and pushed her long brown hair off her shoulders. She started braiding it behind her neck.

"He said it, and he means it," said Mamma.

"He doesn't mean it," sobbed Calvin.

"Do you *mean* it, Mikey?" asked Mamma.

Of course I don't mean it, thought Mikey. "I mean it!"

"Okay." Mamma's voice was final. "Okay. That's over." She cleared her throat. "Now, about this slingshot: I don't want it in the house, Mikey."

"It won't be in the house. I'm bringing it to Iowa."

"Oh no you're not."

"Yes I am." Mikey thought about the small but well-equipped house in Iowa. "You never go in Grandpa's basement, Mamma. He has pictures of himself in the army holding a rifle. Grandpa will love a slingshot."

"Listen, Mikey, I won't have you terrorizing everyone in the car with a slingshot for two days."

"Then I'll pack it." Mikey kept his voice reasonable. "It won't be out in the car. It'll be all packed up."

Mamma looked at the stick on the floor. "Is that branch part of your slingshot?"

"It's a stick. The perfect stick."

"It's a tree," said Victoria. She pulled a ribbon out of her pocket and tied it into the bottom of her braid.

"No big sticks in the car," said Mamma.

Mikey worked at keeping his voice steady. "I said I'd pack it."

"I don't want a dirty stick in the suitcase with my clothes," said Victoria.

"It won't be in the suitcase," said Mikey. "I'll put it in my backpack."

"Mikey, we're all bringing a suitcase," said Mamma softly. "This is a car trip, not a Cub Scout overnight."

"But my backpack is all ready. I packed it."

"You did?"

"Yes. I have three pairs of underpants and three shorts and three shirts and pajamas and a pair of socks." It sounded good, even to Mikey's ears.

"How responsible of you." Mamma glowed. "You knew just what to bring."

Mikey put both hands in his pockets and threw his shoulders back.

"He heard us talking when we packed my stuff," said Victoria.

"He did a fine job, Victoria. Lay off him."

"He didn't bring a bathing suit," said Victoria.

Mamma frowned. "You didn't bring a bathing suit, Mikey?"

Mikey could feel his heartbeat speed up. "I'm not going swimming."

Mamma pursed her lips. "Of course you're going swimming."

"No. I don't like to swim."

"He means he's afraid because he can't swim," said Victoria.

Mikey's hands in his pockets clenched into fists.

"Grandma already signed you up for beginner classes in Iowa." Mamma put her hand on Mikey's arm. "It'll be fun."

Mikey remembered the pool. They had gone there last summer for the free-swim hours in the early evening. There was a big kid who went around dunking people. Mikey called him the Dumb Dunker—not to his face, just inside Mikey's head. The Dumb Dunker swam like a whale, spitting water everywhere. He never dunked Mikey, because Mikey kept his eye on him and quickly got out of the water if he came in Mikey's direction. Would the Dumb Dunker be there again this summer?

But even if he wasn't, the pool was awful. It was so crowded that sometimes Mikey couldn't see his parents sitting on the side. Could he stand taking lessons in that pool? Beginner lessons? "Everyone in the beginner class will be in kindergarten."

"Not everyone," said Mamma. "There will be other children who are bigger."

"Are there any fourth-grade boys?"

"You're not a fourth grader yet," said Victoria.

"Then you're not a sixth grader," said Mikey.

"I guess you could call someone between third and fourth grade a fourth grader," said Victoria, tapping her chin. "Yes, I guess that's exactly what you'd call someone."

Mikey snorted triumphantly. But then he remembered what they were talking about. "I won't take beginner lessons."

"You'll never learn to swim if you don't," said Victoria.

"Who cares?"

"You do," said Victoria.

"I do not," shouted Mikey.

"The lessons will give you confidence," said Mamma. "That's all you need."

Confidence, thought Mikey. How could confidence keep the water from rushing up his nose and down his throat? How could confidence keep the Dumb Dunker from holding him under? How could confidence keep him from drowning? Mikey didn't need confidence. He needed shallow water and good luck.

"Do me and Julie have to take lessons?" asked Calvin.

"They don't give lessons to preschoolers at this pool. Where is Julie anyway?" asked Mamma, looking around.

Julie was sitting on the floor in the corner. She smiled at everyone and stuffed a rubber band down the heating vent.

"Hey! That's my rubber band!" Mikey came around the table toward Julie. "Hey! What did you do with the rest of them?"

"Do rest of dem," said Julie, looking at her empty hands.

"They're all down the heating vent," said Victoria. "I saw her take them off the table."

"I'll kill her!" Mikey lunged for Julie.

"Stop!" Mamma caught Mikey by the arm. "I'm sorry, Mikey. She didn't have any idea what she was doing."

"Victoria knew!"

"Huh?" Victoria shook her head. "It wasn't my fault. I had nothing to do with your stupid rubber bands."

"It was no one's fault," said Mamma. "It was just

bad luck. Look, Mikey, you can bring your backpack, okay? And when we get to Iowa, you can ask Grandpa to help you make a . . . a . . . a pole to fish with. How does that sound?"

Fishing. Mikey imagined himself being pulled into deep water by the only giant shark anyone had ever seen in Iowa, right on the end of his fishing line. Unlucky Mikey. He'd probably drown in Iowa.

2

Getting Ready

The next morning Mikey came downstairs in a yellow shirt with a surfer on the back. That surfer was definitely a good swimmer. He probably took lessons when he was a kid. The very thought of swimming lessons made Mikey feel like going back to bed. Sometimes people took swimming lessons and they never did learn to swim anyway. It was no guarantee.

Mamma smiled as Mikey came into the kitchen. "Do you want cereal?"

"Sure." Mikey went over to the open cupboard.

Calvin sat on the floor beside Yippy and stared

into the cupboard. "No Cheerios. No Rice Chex. No Grape-Nuts."

Mikey checked the cupboard. "There's nothing but shredded wheat. I hate shredded wheat. What the hell is going on?"

"Don't swear, Mikey, please. It's a bad habit. You'll give Grandma a heart attack if you do that in front of her."

Mikey thought of Grandma. A few years ago she'd taken to singing opera songs in the bathroom. Mamma had called it a "peculiar habit," but Mikey liked it. A lot. Grandma had her own ways. He didn't imagine that Grandma would really mind if he swore. But he didn't feel like arguing the point with Mamma. He wanted some decent breakfast. "I don't care. Why don't we have any good cereal?"

"You'd better care." Mamma put a bowl on the table. "There's no other cereal because we're leaving for vacation today. Eat shredded wheat."

"I just told you I hate shredded wheat." Mikey looked at Julie, who was looking at him. In front of her was a half-eaten bowl of Cheerios. "Hey, Julie has Cheerios!"

"Julie was the first one up. She finished the box."

"I wanted to finish the box," said Mikey.

"Here," said Julie. She pushed her bowl toward Mikey's spot, splashing milk on the table.

Mikey looked at Julie's face. There was grape jelly smeared across her nose and one cheek. There was a Cheerio stuck to her chin. And she had a milk mustache. "I don't want your yucky germs," said Mikey. He pushed the bowl back in front of Julie.

"Yucky," said Julie. She made a face at the bowl.

"I'll take it," chirped Calvin. He grabbed the bowl. "I love Julie's germs." He plopped down on the floor and gobbled Cheerios.

Mikey went to the refrigerator. "I'll make myself an egg with melted cheese on top." He felt better already. Mikey loved to cook. He opened the refrigerator door. "There's no eggs! There's no cheese!"

"I don't shop right before going on vacation."

Mikey threw his hands up and stomped to the stairs. "I'll eat later."

He went up to the playroom and closed the door. The playroom was heavenly quiet. Mikey looked around slowly. Everything was neatly organized in its proper place on the shelves. The playroom, unlike the kitchen, was the same as always—well stocked and ready for him. Mikey took a deep breath of relief. He got the box of fluorescent crayons from the top shelf, where he kept it hidden under the construction paper. He clipped a sheet of paper to the easel. What could he draw?

Maybe something for Daddy. Daddy understood the value of a good breakfast. And of a good lunch. And of a good dinner. Daddy loved to eat. Mikey drew a huge blue plate. Then he drew a pile of peas and a lump of meat and a portion of sliced tomatoes. He added brown spots for basil on the tomatoes. He put a glass of beer and a Snickers bar above the plate. He drew an airplane at the top and filled in the sides gray. He printed ICE in black on the gray. Then he drew ice cubes falling from the plane into the beer. Daddy liked his beer cold. Mikey smiled to himself. This picture was looking good.

"Mikey," Mamma called up the stairs. "Wake Victoria, please."

"Sure." Mikey went into the girls' bedroom. He climbed up on Victoria's bunk and shouted in her ear, "Wake up, frog butt."

Victoria groaned and rolled onto her stomach. "Frog butt."

Frog butt was the name Mikey had used for Victoria for the past year, ever since last summer when Mamma said Victoria swam like a fish and Daddy corrected her, saying she swam like a frog. No one ever said Mikey swam like a frog. No one ever would.

Mikey spied something red under the edge of Julie's bureau. He climbed down off the bunk. "We're going to Iowa without you."

"Mmm," said Victoria into her pillow. "Go ahead."

Mikey picked up the red thing. Sure enough, it was a rubber band. He ran into his bedroom and grabbed a Ping-Pong ball. He ran back, spread the index and middle finger of his left hand into a fork, arranged the band and ball, and shot.

The ball hit Victoria on the nose. "Ouch!" she shouted. "I'm going to tell."

Mikey walked back to the playroom. He wished Grandpa could have seen that shot. He stopped in horror in the doorway. There was Calvin sitting at the easel, singing as he worked. "What are you

doing?" Mikey ran up behind Calvin. There were marks all around Daddy's dinner plate. "You've ruined my picture, you jerk! It was a gift for Daddy, and you ruined it."

Calvin started to cry. "I was making it better."

"Better!" Mikey pointed at the dinner plate. "What are all those stupid marks around the plate?"

"They're letters."

"You don't put letters on plates."

"There are letters on my plate," said Calvin, sobbing.

"He's right," said Victoria, coming into the room. She peered at the picture. "Looks more like hieroglyphics to me, though."

"What's that?" asked Calvin.

Hieroglyphics. Victoria always tried to win by bringing up things no one else knew. Well, she was wrong this time. Mikey's third-grade class had studied Egypt. "Dumb Egyptian junk," said Mikey. "I don't want that junk on my drawing!"

"Egyptian writing," said Victoria.

"Who cares what they are?" Mikey made a monster face at Victoria; then he shook the back of Calvin's chair. "You ruined my picture, and now I won't make you one. I'm making one for everyone in the family except you." Mikey pushed Calvin off the chair and sat down at the easel.

"Oh, no," wailed Calvin. "He's making one for everyonc except me. Oh, no."

Victoria put her arm around Calvin. "That's okay, Calvin. I'll make you a picture. I draw better than Mikey anyway."

"Oh no you won't. You swim better than me, but I draw better than you. I'll draw him a picture," said Mikey.

"How can I swim better than you if you don't swim at all?" said Victoria. "That's illogical."

"Eat a fly, frog butt!" Mikey turned to Calvin. "What do you want a picture of, Calvin?"

"Sleep blanket."

"You want a picture of your grimy old blanket?" asked Victoria. "It's almost as ratty as Mikey's."

"Get dressed," said Mikey to Victoria. He grabbed a blue crayon. "Okay, Calvin, hold your blanket up for me. I want to get it perfect."

Everyone was buckled into the car. Daddy switched on the motor. Then he switched it off. "Listen,

Mikey, these pictures you taped to everyone's windows are interesting—"

"Mine's not so interesting," said Victoria. "The giraffe in my picture looks dead. Its neck hangs to one side."

Calvin looked over Victoria's shoulder. "Its tail looks dead, too."

"Dead," said Julie, without looking.

Mikey leaned closer to the drawing. The giraffe didn't look so bad. "It's just a flexible giraffe," said Mikey.

"Flexible?" Victoria looked at Mikey as though he were crazy.

"You know. It's relaxed."

"Whoever heard of a relaxed giraffe? And look, its spots are all smudged," said Victoria, "as though it got wet. Maybe it drowned."

"It didn't drown," said Mikey.

"Maybe it did. Maybe it drowned in a swimming lesson when the teacher wasn't looking."

"That's enough, Victoria," said Mamma. "Your giraffe looks perfectly healthy to me."

Daddy cleared his throat. "Mikey, I appreciate

your pictures, but it's hard to drive when the windows are covered."

"Take them down," said Mikey finally. He chewed at a hangnail on his pinkie. He wouldn't think about a pool full of giraffes, all splashing happily while one was off in a corner quietly drowning.

"You certainly are reasonable these days," said Mamma. "Everyone can look at your pictures when we stop."

Mikey watched as Victoria peeled her giraffe off the window. He turned to look out his own window. "Do you really think your picture's interesting, Dad, or did you just say that?"

"I love it," said Daddy.

Mikey leaned forward. "What do you love about it?"

"Why, I love the strawberries."

"What strawberries?" asked Mikey.

"Aren't these strawberries?" asked Daddy, pointing.

"Those are tomatoes," said Mikey.

"With gnats on them—an outdoor meal," said Victoria.

"There are no gnats on them."

"Yes there are," said Victoria.

"I drew them, frog butt!"

"Then what are those brown specks?" asked Victoria sweetly.

"That's basil! Everybody knows you need basil with tomatoes!"

"I forgot what a chef you are," said Victoria.

"Stop it, you two," said Daddy. "Victoria, do you have to needle him all the time? Show a little respect for your brother."

"And he is a good cook, Victoria," said Mamma. "He makes the best salads of anyone in the family."

"Okay, Dad, let's skip the tomatoes. What else did you like?"

A flash of worry crossed Daddy's face. Then he smiled. "I like this plane. It's dropping ice. Very clever, Mikey."

"You don't put ice in beer," said Victoria. "It melts and ruins the taste."

Daddy hurried on. "And I like these decorations around the plate. They're fascinating."

"Calvin drew those." Mikey flung himself against the back of his seat. "You like what Calvin did!"

"Calvin did those?" Daddy held the drawing up close to his face. "Oh yes, I can see that now. By the way, Calvin, what are they?"

"The alphabet," said Calvin, sitting up tall.

"I see an *A* and a *T* and all these *P*'s. That's very good, Calvin."

"There aren't lots of *P*'s in the alphabet," said Victoria. "There's just one."

"Oh yes there are," said Calvin. "There's many *P*'s."

"Why, Calvin, what gave you that idea?" asked Mamma.

"Everyone knows that," said Calvin. "You say it and my teacher says it and everyone says it."

Mamma spoke carefully. "I never told you there were lots of *P*'s in the alphabet, Calvin."

"Oh yes you did," said Calvin, almost in tears. "You know the song. 'A, B, C, D, E, F, G, H, I, J, K, L, O, many P.' "

Everyone laughed.

Julie clapped. "Smart Calvin," she said. "Smart Calvin."

"Calvin, it's 'L, M, N, O, P,' " said Daddy. "We can work on that tonight when we stop."

Calvin was silent. His eyes showed confusion and disappointment. He turned to face the rear again. Mikey was silent, too. He thought of the speckled sliced tomatoes that looked like strawberries, the melting ice in the beer, the drowned giraffe. He glanced over at Victoria. She looked at him sadly and whispered, "They always praise you, not me. I'm a good cook, too."

Yippy barked as Daddy backed the car down the driveway.

3

Ice Cream

They were on the road three hours before they stopped and ate lunch. Then they headed for the ice-cream bar.

Victoria ordered first: "Mint chocolate chip."

Mikey watched Victoria take a bite. The green ice cream was the color of coolness. And there were so many chips. He looked at the list of flavors. Some of them were bound to be terrible. Some of them might be good, though. Some of them might be fabulous. On the other hand, he could always count on vanilla.

"Mikey, it's your turn," said Mamma.

"Vanilla," said Mikey. "No, I don't know. Do Calvin next."

"Raspberry sherbet," said Calvin. "I love pink."

"Mikey?" said Daddy.

Mikey had read about halfway through the list of ice-cream flavors. "Mocha chip," he said slowly.

"Mocha chip is coffee with chocolate chips," said Daddy.

"I don't want that," said Mikey. "Ask Julie first."

"Julie wants vanilla," said Mamma.

"Why does she always want vanilla?" asked Mikey.

"Because it's easier to wash out of her clothes," said Victoria.

"That's not fair!" Mikey glared at his mother. "She should pick for herself, just like the rest of us."

Daddy held Julie up. "Okay, Julie, what do you want?"

"Dat," said Julie, pointing at Calvin's raspberry cone. "Dat," she said, pointing at Victoria's mint chocolate chip.

"How about something new? Peach for Julie," ordered Daddy.

Everyone turned to Mikey.

"Pistachio," said Mikey.

"You've never had it before," said Victoria. "It stinks."

"Pistachio? Are you sure?" said Mamma.

Mikey didn't feel sure of anything. Maybe Victoria was saying pistachio stank because it was wonderful and she didn't want him to have something wonderful. Anyway, he couldn't have vanilla all the time. Even Julie was having something new. "Yes."

The ice-cream lady handed Mikey a green cone. It smelled yucky. He licked it. It tasted awful.

Daddy got fudge walnut. He bit right into it. Mamma got vanilla, but she didn't lick it. She looked at Mikey. "Green is my favorite color," said Mamma. "How's your green cone, Mikey?"

"It's okay." Mikey wrinkled his nose without meaning to.

"I like pistachio, you know."

Mikey didn't want to let his mother rescue him in front of Victoria. But he didn't want to have to eat that awful cone. "If you like green best, I'm willing to trade."

"Thanks." Mamma traded cones with Mikey.

They walked outside. Victoria moved closer to Mikey. "I knew you'd hate it," she said. "You have trouble making decisions, Mikey. It's part of your lack of confidence, like Mamma says. It's what makes you afraid of everything."

"I'm not afraid of anything."

"What about swimming?"

"I'm not afraid, frog butt. I'm unlucky. Unlucky people drown."

"You're afraid," said Victoria. "That's your problem."

"Your ice cream has gnats on it. That's your problem."

"They aren't gnats," said Victoria. "They're chocolate chips."

"They look like gnats."

Mamma and Daddy stood by the car, talking over an open map. The children sat in the grass and ate their ice cream.

"Mine was excellent." Victoria lay back.

"Mine is perfect." Mikey licked slowly. "Perfect."

"I love mine," said Calvin, crunching up the cone.

They looked around for Julie. She sat on the grass beside Yippy. She gave Yippy a lick of her cone. Then she took a lick.

Victoria rolled her eyes. "How disgusting!"

"Yuck!" said Mikey.

Mamma walked over quickly. She took the cone and gave it to Yippy. She looked at her watch. "There's no time to stand in line and get another cone. Who wants to share with Julie?"

Everyone looked at Mikey, the only one left with a cone.

"No." Mikey looked at the ground. "Just because everyone else in the family is a fast eater, that doesn't mean I should be the one who has to share."

Mamma stared at Mikey. "She'd share with you."

Mikey took a lingering lick. He looked at Julie. Her face was covered with ice cream. Her hands were a mixture of ice cream and dirt. She must have had at least a thousand germs on her nose alone. Julie looked at Mikey with big, pleading eyes. The poor little piggy. "Oh, all right," said Mikey. "How about if I eat down to the cone and then give the rest to her?"

"Good solution," said Daddy.

Mikey ate down to the cone. He took one last long lick. Then he handed the rest to Julie. She walked over to Yippy and dropped the cone on the grass. "Eat," she said as Yippy pounced.

4

The Motel

Victoria squirmed. Yippy lay asleep across her lap with her paws between Victoria's knees. Mikey watched Victoria out of the corner of his eye. Then he carefully fitted another gun barrel into the front of the paper model of a Sherman tank that he'd been working on since their last stop. He sneaked another peek at Victoria. He knew that Yippy's nails were digging into her leg. He knew that Victoria was afraid of moving the dog because Mamma had said that once Yippy woke up, Victoria's turn would be over and Mikey would get the dog.

Victoria moved her knees slightly. Yippy's head popped up.

"Hey, it's my turn to have Yippy." Mikey cleared the paper model off his lap.

"But I've only had her five minutes," said Victoria.

"You've had her longer than that," Mikey said.

"No I haven't. Just look at my watch."

Mikey looked at the watch. "How does that prove anything? It's seven-thirty. So what?"

"Do you know what time it was when I got Yippy?"

Mikey could feel himself being drawn into a trap, but he didn't know exactly what the trap was. "No," he said doubtfully.

"So if you don't know what time it was when I got Yippy, then you can't know how long I've had her."

"That's stupid. I know how long you've had her."

"How?" asked Victoria.

"I have a good sense of time."

"All right, smarty. Then look out the window and tell me when five minutes are up."

Mikey looked out the window. Five minutes was about as long as it took him to ride his bike to school. Daddy had clocked him once. He was the fastest bike rider around. Everyone else who started with him arrived after he did. Mikey imagined himself riding his bike. Just about now he'd be passing the library. And now he'd be zooming down Martin Place, right up to the back of the school. "Time's up," he shouted.

"Ha!" Victoria held out her watch. "You started at seven thirty-three and it's only seven thirty-five. Ha-ha-ha!"

Mikey leaned across the baggage on the seat and stretched out his arm. Victoria was just out of pinching reach. He swung his hand as hard as he could and barely caught her shoulder with his fingertips.

"Mikey hit me," said Victoria. "Mamma, Mikey hit me."

Daddy spoke up suddenly. "No hitting and no teasing. You make each other feel bad. Both of you say sorry."

"I'm sorry," said Mikey woodenly.

"I'm sorry, Mikey," said Victoria. "I didn't do anything wrong, but I'm sorry you feel bad."

"She doesn't mean it," said Mikey.

"Time to head for a motel," said Daddy.

"Who's going to get us ice?" Mamma picked up the ice bucket and held it out.

"I am," shouted Mikey.

"I am," shouted Victoria.

Yippy barked.

"We've got to try to stay calm and quiet so Yippy doesn't bark," said Daddy. "I mean it, kids."

"Sure," said Mikey. It would get dark soon, and the motel was big. Maybe going with Victoria would be a good idea. "We can get ice together, right, Victoria?"

Victoria picked up the Gideon Bible off the night-stand. She rubbed the cover thoughtfully. "You go get the ice, Mikey." She opened the Bible. "Come here, Calvin. I'm going to read to you about the beginning of time."

"Oh, goody! I love the beginning of time." Calvin ran over and plopped down beside Victoria on the bed.

Mikey took the ice bucket and went out. He looked at the number over their room door: 8A. That was simple to remember. Mikey went to the right. At the end of the corridor there was no choice; he went left. He swung the ice bucket and reminded himself that it was easy to get back to the room. He looked over his shoulder. The hall was deserted.

Maybe the whole motel was deserted except for his family. He walked faster. How far was the ice machine?

A door opened right behind him.

Mikey moved closer to the wall and walked on, looking straight ahead. What if someone mean came out of the room and beat him up? Or even killed him? Would his family miss him? Would Victoria be sorry she'd been so mean to him all his life? Mikey held the rim of the ice bucket so tight his fingers hurt.

A person stepped out into the hall and walked quickly behind him.

Mikey thought of running. But no kid his age could outrun a healthy adult. In a situation like this you had to use your wits. You had to act fast. The surprise element was all-important. In one motion, Mikey turned and threw the bucket into the air, screaming, "Ice!"

The bucket clattered against the wall and rolled into the center of the hall right in front of the person. It was a tall woman. Openmouthed, she stared at Mikey. In one hand she held an ice bucket. She reached down, keeping her eyes on Mikey, and

22 A

picked up his bucket. "Did you say ice?" she asked weakly.

Mikey took the bucket and nodded. He tried to speak, but no words came out. He flattened himself against the wall and wished he could disappear through it.

"I think it's this way." She smiled uncertainly and took a few steps. "Aren't you coming?"

"Yup," croaked Mikey. He slowly followed her.

The woman's face twitched. She walked ahead, looking over her shoulder twice. When she reached the middle of the hall, she disappeared to the left. She emerged a moment later with a full bucket of ice. She smiled cautiously and went past Mikey back to her room.

Mikey waited a moment after she was gone. There was no one else around. Thank heavens. At least no one had seen him act so stupid. He walked ahead faster now. The ice machine stood in a little lighted room with other machines. Mikey filled the bucket, then explored the machines.

The first had candy. The next one had pop. Mikey turned to the last machine. It displayed a pocket compass, a miniature tube of lipstick, a pair of dice in a transparent plastic ball, a tiny folding knife, and a black plastic wallet. He looked at the sign on the machine. Seventy-five cents.

For seventy-five cents Mikey could have his own folding knife. He could whittle with a knife. His neighbor Ben had whittled a whistle last summer. He could clean fish with a knife. Hadn't Mamma said that he could go fishing with Grandpa? He could throw a knife at a target on a pine tree. Victoria could never do that with her lousy aim. There were a hundred things Mikey could do with a knife. A hundred and twenty, even. He needed that knife.

Mikey took the ice bucket and started back for the room. He stopped. What if the same woman should come out of her room again? Mikey's cheeks burned at the thought. He could get back to his room by another route, simply by making a big loop in the other direction. He went to the end of the corridor and turned left. Then at the end of that one he turned left again. He was surprised to find that there were rooms on only the left side now. On the right was a railing, and over the railing he could see a courtyard with a large pool.

There was a family in the pool. A boy sat on the

side and kicked his legs in the water. He must have been about six. Mikey watched as he splashed his father, then his mother. There were no other children. An only child. An only child who probably was never told he had to give half his ice-cream cone to anyone.

The father went across the pool from the boy, and the mother got out of the water. She sneaked up behind the boy. Mikey's eyes widened. The mother pushed. They were going to kill the boy! Mikey screamed, "Murder!" The boy swam to his father, swinging his arms wildly. The father looked up at Mikey with bewilderment on his face. He waved.

Mikey ran down the corridor to the end, turned left, and ran till he found 8A. He pounded on the door.

"Finally," said Daddy. "We were about to search for you. What happened?"

Mikey didn't think he wanted to talk about everything that had happened. In fact, he didn't want to talk about any of it. He held out the bucket silently.

"Thanks," said Mamma.

Mikey looked around. They all had their bathing suits on. Oh, no.

"Get your suit on, Mikey," said Daddy. "We're taking a dip."

"I didn't bring a suit." Mikey walked past Daddy and turned on the TV. He didn't dare look his parents in the eye. "I'll stay here and watch TV."

"There's a suit in your backpack." Mamma spoke normally, as though it was no big deal. "I added it this morning."

"You had no right to do that! I didn't want it!"

"You can stay in the shallow end."

Mikey swung on the steel handrail that went down the three steps into the pool. He pulled his knees up so that he could clear the steps as he swung. Mikey looked around at his family.

Victoria bounced a few times on the diving board. Then she cannonballed with a big splash. Mamma swung Calvin in an arc, back and forth through the water, holding him under the arms. He laughed and laughed.

Julie picked leaves off the bushes in the courtyard and brought them over to the pool steps. "Food," she said. "Eat."

Mikey pretended to munch on the leaves. He

wondered why Julie had such a passion for feeding others. "Tasty leaves," he said. He felt good. When they had first come down to the pool, he had expected to find the other family still there. He had expected everyone to watch that little kid swim across the pool. He had expected them to say what a great swimmer that six-year-old was. And he'd have said it was maybe a small seven-year-old. Maybe a midget eight-year-old. And they'd have laughed at him. Victoria would have called him jealous.

But when they came down, the pool was empty. And now everyone was having fun, and no one was paying any attention to Mikey. No one but Julie. Mikey turned onto his stomach and lay on the steps. He held his body stiff and balanced on his arms. He put his face in the water and blew bubbles.

"That's great work, Mikey," came Daddy's voice from behind him. "You remember a lot about swimming from last summer, don't you?"

Mikey turned over and looked at his father. "Dad, was Victoria really only five when she learned how to swim?"

"Mmm-hmm. She learned in the summer, right before she turned six."

"I'm nine." Mikey looked off at some distant point.

"Do you remember when you learned to ride your bike, Mikey?"

"Sure," said Mikey. "I was black and blue all summer." He laughed.

"Yeah. You were a mess. But Victoria didn't get any bruises when she learned. She was careful, because she didn't want to get hurt. You weren't afraid of being hurt at all." Daddy spoke very quietly. "You weren't afraid then, Mikey. So why are you so afraid of swimming?"

"You don't die when you fall off a bike." Mikey sighed. "Now Victoria can swim and she can ride a bike, too."

"Victoria turned eight that summer."

"Yeah."

"Did you hear me, Mikey? Victoria turned eight when she learned to ride a bike, but you weren't even four and a half when you learned."

"Hey, yeah." Mikey sat upright on the top step now. "I was faster than her on riding a bike, and she's faster than me on swimming." Mikey stopped. Then he added doubtfully, "Maybe I'll learn to swim this year."

"You're sure starting right. Blowing bubbles and floating are the first steps, and you already know them perfectly. All you have to do is put an arm stroke in there, and you'll be off and away." Daddy dipped under the water and came up all wet. Water dripped off his hair into his eyes. He looked slightly like a seal. "I've got a secret to tell you, Mikey. A secret that you know already, down in your heart." He was whispering. "Most people are afraid of swimming at first. The point is not to let the fear stop you from learning." He flipped over onto his back and looked up into the sky.

Mikey let himself slide down to the third step, so that he was chest-deep in water. He put both arms straight out in front of him. This much he could do; he knew he could. He pulled his right arm back toward his chest, then lifted it out of the water and stretched it out straight again. Then he pulled his left arm back and did the same thing.

"Hey, you already know an arm stroke. That's a great one," said Daddy.

"Victoria taught me. It's the arms for the American crawl." Mikey stopped. "Dad . . ."

"What is it, Mikey?"

"Every time I see deep water, I think I'll drown."

"Daddy, Daddy, watch me!" Victoria stood on the diving board, and the last rays of sunlight sparkled on her wet legs. She dived.

Mikey watched the spot on the surface of the water where her feet had disappeared. Victoria was gone from sight, under all that water, but she'd come up again in a moment, laughing and snorting water. Under and up.

"Help!"

Mikey saw Calvin lose hold of the side of the pool, just a few feet from him. He froze. The water closed over Calvin's head. But he didn't come up. In an instant the world went silent. Mikey knew where everyone was—Daddy, on the steps; Victoria, surfacing from her dive; Mamma, in a metal chair; Julie, in the bushes—but he couldn't hear any of them. He couldn't move. He couldn't breathe. It was as though he was on the bottom, rather than Calvin. Mikey, under tons of water. Under, but never to come up again.

"Help!" This time it was Mikey shouting. Then the air was full of noise again. And Daddy was grabbing Calvin and lifting him out onto the side. And

Mamma was hugging him and rubbing his arms. And Victoria was climbing out and dripping over him. And Julie was shoving leaves in his face. Everyone talked at once. Only a few seconds had passed.

Mikey stood on the pool steps. He clutched the metal railing tight and watched the crowd around his brother.

That night Daddy and Mikey worked with Calvin on the alphabet. Later, when Daddy kissed Mikey good-night, he whispered in his ear, "You won't drown, Mikey. Not ever."

"Calvin almost drowned today."

"No he didn't. He went under, but there were lots of people around to save him."

"I couldn't have saved him."

"Yes you could. The water there only came up to your chest, at most. You can do more than you think you can."

"I was afraid. I couldn't move."

"And you were right. Mamma and I were there to do it. But if you had been alone, you'd have reached out a hand and pulled Calvin to safety."

"I might have drowned with him."

"Not in water that shallow. But if it had been deeper, you could have thrown him a life preserver. There was one hanging on the fence behind the lifeguard's chair."

"I don't know if I could think that fast."

"You could. In an emergency you'd find a way to stay safe and still help. You'd stand on the side and extend a stick or a piece of clothing or something. And you'd call for help, the way you did today."

"Yeah, I could call for help."

"And someone would come."

"Someone would come."

"Yes, someone would surely come."

Mikey closed his eyes and listened to Calvin's heavy breathing in the bed beside him. He remembered the silence when Calvin had gone under. No sound. No breath. No breath in that horrible, cold moment. He touched Calvin's hand. It was warm and soft. Calvin squirmed and rolled over. Mikey opened his eyes and stared through the darkness at nothing.

5

The Knife

"I'm using the bathroom now." Victoria shoved the door closed.

Mikey shoved back harder and stuck in his head.

Victoria let go of the door with a huff and ran her brush through her hair.

"I want to tell you something," Mikey whispered.

Victoria screwed up her mouth. "What is it?"

"Shh." Mikey slipped in and shut the door. "There's a wonderful machine down the hall. It costs seventy-five cents."

Victoria whispered, "The machine costs seventy-five cents?"

"My knife."

"The machine sells knives?"

"And lipstick."

"I like lipstick. What else?"

"A compass, a wallet, and dice."

"Let's ask Mamma for money."

"You do it," said Mikey.

"Why me?"

"'Cause if I do it, she'll ask what for, and she won't let me get a knife."

Victoria nodded. "But if you get it, she'll find out you have it. Then she'll take it away anyway."

"Maybe she won't find out."

"She will."

"Maybe she won't."

"She will."

"Go ask for the money, Victoria."

"All right."

They brushed their teeth; then they came out of the bathroom trying to look as though nothing special was up. Mikey sat on the bed nearest the bathroom while Victoria went to Mamma.

"Mamma, Mikey and I want to buy gifts for all the kids. There's a machine down the hall. It only costs seventy-five cents. Can I have twelve quarters?"

"The toys that come out of those machines break in a flash." Mamma set bagels and cream cheese on a towel spread out on the floor. "Help me prepare breakfast."

Mikey looked at Victoria with desperation in his eyes.

Victoria knelt beside her mother and unwrapped the cheese. "We need treats for the car. Calvin and Julie can get theirs when they're feeling bored. Surprises help with cranky children."

Mikey breathed deeply and watched his mother.

"You may have a good idea there." Mamma sat back on her heels. "Okay, I guess. After breakfast you can go get them."

"Can I have the money now?" Victoria put out napkins.

"Take three dollar bills from my purse and run down to the motel office for change. Do you remember where the office is?"

"Of course." Victoria took the money and left.

Mamma turned to Daddy. "How about if we take a morning swim?"

Daddy sat down at the breakfast towel. "I like to hit the road early." He took a bagel and spread cream cheese on it.

Mikey quietly bit into his own bagel and looked at the floor. Yippy came up behind him and begged. Mikey pushed the pup away and ate faster. Yippy took the edge of Mikey's pajama top in her teeth and tugged. Mikey toppled over and wrestled with the dog. He could feel Daddy's eyes on him.

"On second thought," Daddy said, "we all enjoyed ourselves last night in the pool. A swim now might be nice. What do you think, Mikey?"

Mikey sat up and finished his last bite of bagel. His father's eyes were hopeful. Mikey remembered the three steps and the steel rail. He could stand it. "Sure, Dad."

Mikey was back at his old spot in the pool. This time he was on his back with both arms under him touching the second step. "Watch me, Victoria. When I keep my legs straight, my toes pop up. Even when I try to keep them under, they pop up."

"Ha! Think what would happen if you didn't try to keep them down. They might fly up out of the water and you'd be hanging upside down in midair." Victoria laughed.

Mikey imagined himself rising upside down. What if his toes didn't fly up far enough and his head stayed underwater? He sat up. Goose bumps formed on his chest and shoulders.

"Want to go to your machine now?" Victoria got out of the water and stood dripping and shivering by the steps.

"Sure."

They grabbed towels and ran for the glass doors. It was cold in the dark corridor. "There it is." Mikey stood in the doorway and pointed. Victoria handed Mikey his three quarters in silence. He put them in and pulled the lever.

The knife had no box or plastic wrapping. It hit the tray of the machine with a clink. Closed like that, the knife was about the length of Mikey's index finger, but narrower. It was black. Mikey checked the machine. The knife in the display was tan. Mikey looked at the one in his hand. Black was much better than tan.

Victoria moved closer to him. "Open it."

Mikey opened it, and they both felt the blade. It

PRIZES
PRIZES
75¢
POOL

was coarse and thick, like the blades on Calvin's scissors. But it had a sharp point, and the chrome was shiny.

"I'm going to whittle with it," Mikey whispered.

Victoria licked her lips. "I'm going to get the compass."

"I thought you'd want the lipstick."

"Well, it's a close choice, but the compass wins. Maybe I'll get Calvin the lipstick. Then if it isn't pink, he'll give it to me anyway."

"Then let's get Julie the wallet and she can give it to me."

They carried the toys outside, where everyone else was just getting out of the pool. Mikey hid the knife in his towel. He ran through the bushes, searching for the right piece of wood to whittle. "Hey, Mamma," he called, "can me and Victoria sit in the back and let Julie and Calvin sit in the middle?"

"Victoria and I, not me and Victoria," said Mamma. "Changing seats just throws everyone off, Mikey. Two-year-olds don't like change. Julie will feel confused."

"No, she won't," said Calvin. "I'll take care of her.

I want to sit in the middle with Yippy on my lap."

"Oh, all right. Let's just hurry and go."

During the next two hours in the car Mikey whittled. He'd had no idea how difficult it would be. No matter what position he held the wood in, no matter what position he held the knife in, all he could make were ragged gouges like claw marks.

"This is damn hard," Mikey whispered to Victoria.

"I know. I've been watching you." Victoria ran her finger along one of the bigger grooves in the wood. "Watch out. You're going to cut yourself if you're not careful."

"Shh!" Mikey looked over his shoulder. He whispered, "Don't talk so loud."

Victoria hissed back, "Mamma's going to find out anyway."

"She won't if you don't tell her."

"Can we stop soon?" Calvin asked suddenly. "I feel sick."

"What? Why?" asked Mamma.

"It's just Yippy." Calvin sat in his car seat with Yippy sprawled across his lap, her paws hanging down on one side.

"What about Yippy?" asked Mamma.

"Her paws smell like popcorn. They make me sick."

"They do?" Mikey unbuckled himself, got on his knees, and leaned over the backseat into the middle seat. "Let me smell them." He sniffed loudly. "They do. You're right. What a terrific dog we have!"

"Put your seat belt back on, Mikey. Calvin, pass Yippy to Julie, and open your window more." Mamma pointed to the road sign. "Let's stop at this rest area."

Daddy guided Calvin with a hand on his shoulder. He opened the bathroom door.

"I'm not sick anymore. Go away. I can go to the bathroom by myself." Calvin shoved Daddy out the door.

Calvin went past the sinks and into the first stall.

Mikey went into the next stall. When he came out, he opened his knife and wiped the blade clean with a paper towel. He folded it shut. "Hey, Calvin. You still in there, bird doo?"

"I can't get the toilet to flush."

"Here, I'll help." Mikey pushed on the stall door. It wasn't latched. Calvin stood beside the toilet with both hands on the flush lever. Mikey leaned across him.

"No, don't help me. I'll do it myself," Calvin yelped. Mikey's left hand was already on the lever. His right held the knife. Calvin pushed straight into Mikey's left side at the very moment that Mikey managed to flush. Mikey fell toward the toilet and caught himself with his right hand on the seat. His knife dropped into the water with a splash. It glistened for an instant.

Then it was gone.

Calvin looked at Mikey's face. "What was it?"

Mikey didn't answer. His face felt heavy.

Calvin's eyes got big and worried. "What? Tell me."

Mikey shook his head and stared at the toilet.

"I'm sorry, I'm sorry, I'm sorry." Calvin burst into tears. "I'm sorry, Mikey. I'm sorry, I'm sorry."

Mikey kept expecting there to be a glint in the bottom of the bowl again. Nothing. He looked slowly at his sobbing brother. He felt numb. "It's okay, Calvin," he said in a hoarse whisper. "I was pretty bad at whittling anyway."

Mikey and Calvin came out of the men's room with glum faces.

Victoria was heading for the women's room. "What happened to you two?"

"My knife's gone," said Mikey.

"Gone where?"

Mikey looked at Calvin. "Just gone."

"I'm sorry," said Victoria. "Too bad." She looked around. "Listen, there must be machines like that all over the place. We'll find another one."

"Yeah," said Mikey without enthusiasm. Then he added with a tiny smile, "Anyway, you were wrong. Mamma never found out."

6

The First Night

"Grandpa's in the garden!" Mikey unbuckled himself and climbed across the middle seat to lean out Calvin's window.

"Grandpa!" yelled Calvin as he pushed Mikey off him.

"Grandpa!" yelled Victoria, climbing into the middle seat and stepping on Yippy, who barked and jumped back and forth.

"Grandpa!" yelled Julie at Victoria's back.

Grandpa stood near the fence of purple pea flowers with his back to the driveway. "He can't hear us," said Mikey. As soon as the car had stopped, Mikey jumped out, ran up to Grandpa, and pulled

on his shirt. Grandpa turned around with a big smile.
"Grandpa, we're here!" Mikey gave Grandpa a bear hug.

Everyone else followed. Kisses flew. Yippy barked and ran in circles, jumping on everyone in turn.

Grandpa turned up the dial on the side of his glasses. That made his hearing aid work better. "So glad you're here!"

Grandma stood quietly at the kitchen door watching the hubbub. Mikey caught her eye. He went quickly into her arms, happy to have her all to himself, even if just for a moment.

"How are you, Grandma?"

"Just fine, sweetie."

"Are you still singing?"

Grandma smiled. "More than ever. I'm taking lessons. And now that Grandpa is so deaf, I can practice anywhere I want. I don't have to shut myself up in the bathroom anymore."

Mikey laughed.

"There's Grandma," yelled Calvin.

The crowd raced over, and Grandma collected kisses all around. Then she led them inside.

"You got a new TV, Grandpa," shouted Mikey into his grandfather's ear. "Let's try it out."

Grandpa picked up the remote control and handed it to Mikey. "You test it out," he said as he sank into his favorite chair.

After dinner Grandma handed a full container of butterball cookies to Mikey. "Take them outside and share them with everyone while your folks and I clean up."

Mikey went out into the yard with everyone following him. He felt like the Pied Piper. He handed out two butterballs to each person.

"Give me another." Victoria chomped on a butterball and held out her hand.

There were still a lot of butterballs left. And they were small. Three seemed like a fair number. So Mikey handed out a third to everyone.

Victoria gobbled hers down. She stuck out her hand. "Another."

Mikey held the container to his chest. "No. You've already had three."

"I want another."

"Everybody gets three."

"I want another, too," said Calvin.

"Me too," said Julie.

Mikey shook his head and held the container even tighter. "Three's enough."

"You're not the boss," said Calvin.

"Grandma said I was in charge."

"Mamma," Victoria shouted as she got up. "Mikey's being bossy."

The word *bossy* stung Mikey. He'd always considered Victoria the bossy one. "You better tell her Grandma put me in charge. You just better tell her!" Mikey shouted.

Victoria went into the kitchen.

"Look." Calvin pointed at Julie.

Julie pulled off the last of her clothes. "Hot," she said. Her whole body glistened with sweat. She put her clothes in a pile and did a gallop dance around the birdbath.

Mikey suddenly remembered the plastic wading pool that Grandpa had bought last summer. It would be perfect on this hot night.

Victoria came out of the house. She swung her

arms and took big, bold steps. "Mamma said we're supposed to work it out ourselves. Give me another butterball or I'll punch your face in."

Mikey put the butterball container on the picnic table. "Remember Grandpa's wading pool?"

"Mmm-hmm." Victoria opened the container and stuffed a butterball into her mouth. "A nice pool on a hot night. That would feel great."

Calvin grabbed a butterball and joined Julie dancing around the birdbath. He sang his favorite song. "Twinkle, twinkle, little star . . ."

When he finished, Julie began. She sang over and over again, "Row, row, row, row . . ." That's all she knew of her favorite song.

"Hey, Grandpa." Mikey leaned over the arm of Grandpa's chair. "Where's the pool?"

"Huh? You're cool?" asked Grandpa.

"The pool, Grandpa," Mikey shouted. "Where's the pool you bought us last summer? We want to play in the pool!"

"Oh, the pool." Grandpa stood up and stretched. "Yes, I've still got that pool. It's in the rafters of the garage."

Mikey helped Grandpa get the pool down from the rafters. Grandpa handed Mikey the hose nozzle and turned on the water.

"When you're through, put the hose away, okay?" Grandpa said as he went into the house.

Mikey filled the pool. Then he turned off the spigot on the side of the house. He looped the hose over his arm many times and set it on the ground beside the garage.

When he turned around, what he saw made him stop short.

Julie stood in the pool and pulled on Yippy's collar. The dog sat in the water. She wouldn't budge. "Come, baby dog," said Julie. She held the container of butterballs in her left arm. She leaned toward the dog, and Yippy stuck her head into the container. "Eat," said Julie happily. "Eat, baby dog."

Victoria ran into the house, shouting, "Mamma!"

Mikey ran over to the pool and grabbed the container from Julie. Only two butterballs remained. "You hairy pig!" he shouted at the dog. "How the hell did you eat them all so fast? Pig!"

Mamma came out the screen door. "Throw out the rest of the cookies. And empty the pool. Dogs are dirty. You can't go in the pool now that she's been in it."

"But, Mamma," said Mikey, "she's just a puppy. She's clean."

"No she's not."

"Yes she is."

"Dogs are never clean," said Mamma. "No arguing. Anyway, it's too late to be playing. You need to get ready for bed. Your swimming lessons start early tomorrow morning."

Mikey went to the pool and pushed down the side of it, so the water poured out. Yippy stayed put in the center of the pool, watching. "I don't want swimming lessons."

"Let's not start that again."

"Why can't we just go to the pool at family hour? Then I'd learn how to swim naturally."

"That's what we did last year—and all you did was blow bubbles for two weeks."

"But, Mamma—"

"No."

Mikey stood at the screen door in his pajamas and looked with curiosity at the huge man in the rubber boots who was talking with Daddy. Victoria and Calvin crowded beside him.

"Come on out," said Daddy. "Meet my old high school buddy Ray."

The three of them came out.

"That's a fine troop." Ray gave them a big, friendly smile. "Bring them over to the farm tomorrow, why don't you?"

"That'd be terrific. The kids are signed up for swimming lessons in the morning, but the afternoon's okay."

"We could skip the lessons," said Mikey.

"Oh, I wouldn't ask you to do that, little fellow," said Ray. "I bet you're a regular fish in the water." He playfully mussed up Mikey's hair and smiled past him at Victoria. "Your father sure has pretty kids for such an ugly old man."

Daddy brushed back his graying hair and laughed.

Calvin looked up at Daddy. "Daddy's old," he half whispered.

"I think you're handsome, Daddy." Victoria moved near Daddy.

Ray smiled again. "I've got to go. Just stopped by because I heard you were getting in today. See you at the farm around one?" Ray pointed at the children. "And stay in swimsuits after the lessons. We've got a nice cool watering hole you can jump in."

"Is it deep?" Mikey blurted out.

"Not deep enough to satisfy a fish like you." Ray scratched his chin. "Must be six, seven feet at the deepest. But you can swim in it. Catch tadpoles at the edge. Maybe a snake even."

"I love snakes," said Calvin.

Mikey tried not to think about the deep part. He could stay on the edge and catch a snake to put under Victoria's pillow.

"That sounds great," said Daddy, throwing his arm around Mikey's shoulders. "And, Ray, I'm sorry about your dad. Wish I could have been here for the funeral."

"Eighty-four years old. We're grateful he didn't suffer. Wasn't sick a day in his life." Ray climbed into his truck.

Daddy nodded. "That's good clean living for you."

"There's nothing clean about farm living." Ray stuck out a muddy rubber boot and pointed. He grinned. "You'll see more of this muck tomorrow. Wear old shoes." He shut the truck door.

They watched the truck drive off. Then they went inside.

Mamma sat on the couch. Julie was asleep on her lap. Mamma smiled contentedly and looked up. Grandpa sat in his favorite living room chair with the newspaper spread across his knees. His eyes were half closed. Grandma sat on the couch beside Mamma and Julie, reading a skinny little book she called a libretto. It was filled with Italian opera songs. Her shoulders and neck moved, as though she was singing silently to herself.

Both Grandma and Grandpa wore red terry-cloth robes. The skin on their faces and hands looked pale and lifeless beside the red. Mikey felt shocked at the realization of how old they were. Maybe they were in their eighties, like Ray's father, who died. He hoped his thoughts didn't show on his face. He suddenly wanted to kiss them both. He wanted to hold them and stop them from growing any older. He walked toward Grandma.

In that instant Calvin ran past Mikey and sat down on the other side of Grandma. He tapped Grandma on the arm urgently. "Grandma, that man said Daddy's old. But you're older. Why aren't you dead?"

"What?" said Grandma. She dropped her libretto.

"Grandma isn't that old, and Daddy isn't that old," said Mamma quickly. "Time for bed, kids." Mamma marched them off to Daddy's old bedroom.

Mikey could hear Grandma's laughter as he pulled up the covers.

7

The Swimming Lesson

"Daddy." Calvin stood beside the open sofa bed in the living room where his parents were sleeping. "I'm hungry."

"Go back to bed."

Mikey watched from the bedroom. It was too early to wake up. He shut his eyes.

"Daddy! Wake up! I'm hungry."

"Calvin," sang Grandma. Her voice rang out from the kitchen.

Mikey struggled out of his sleeping bag and stood groggily in the bedroom doorway.

Grandma came into the living room and smiled at Calvin. She was dressed all in white today, with artificial flowers pinned in her hair. "Can I make you boys some eggs?"

"Cereal for me," said Mikey. He went to the cupboard and looked across the wide selection with satisfaction. He took out a box of Kix. Calvin sat down at the table beside Mikey.

"Would you like an egg?" Grandma repeated.

"Where's Grandpa?" said Calvin.

"He went for a walk." Grandma leaned over Calvin's seat from the side and spoke in a very quiet voice. "Calvin, what can I fix you for breakfast?"

"He went for a walk without me?" Calvin pushed back his chair. "I better go find him."

"Get your bathing suit on before you go outside, Calvin," said Mamma. She stood in the doorway in her nightgown. "I'll take you to the wading pool during the big kids' lessons."

Mikey looked quickly at his mother, ready to protest. She held up her hand in a halt signal. Mikey ate another spoonful of Kix.

Calvin ran to the bedroom. He ran back into the kitchen a moment later. "Where's my bathing suit?" He hopped from one foot to another. "I have to rush to catch up with Grandpa."

"All your things are in the third drawer," said Mamma.

Calvin ran back to the bedroom, Mamma went into the bathroom, and Grandma went down the basement steps with a load of laundry. Mikey sat at the kitchen table alone. He stirred his cereal listlessly.

Calvin came running into the kitchen, still in his pajamas, with something under his arm. He dashed out the back door.

Mikey heard Yippy's hoarse bark of greeting to Calvin as the puppy strained at the rope that tied her to the tree. Mikey took another spoonful of cereal and sloshed it around in his mouth. Suddenly he heard Calvin shout at Yippy. Yippy barked madly. Mikey went to the kitchen door and looked out.

"You killed it!" Calvin screamed. "I hate you, Yippy! I hate you," he sobbed. He hit Yippy on the head with a green cloth.

The dog jumped up and took the cloth in her teeth.

Calvin pulled back. "No, bad dog. Bad, terrible, ugly, bad dog!" Tears streamed down his face.

Yippy jumped around wildly, playing tug-of-war. Calvin fell backward.

"Daddy, Daddy," screamed Calvin.

Mikey went out the door, but Grandpa came around the corner of the house and reached Calvin faster.

"What's the matter, Calvin?" Grandpa spoke gently as he picked Calvin up from behind.

"Yippy killed a baby bird." Calvin sobbed against Grandpa's chest.

Mikey came closer and stood beside Grandpa. They looked at the mess of feathers. It was as though the bird had been nothing more than feathers and feet and a beak. Alive and happy one moment, then gone—totally gone—the next. "How awful," whispered Mikey. He looked up at the spreading shade tree and spied the nest. There were at least two other baby birds there. Maybe three. Mikey hugged himself and shivered.

Grandpa put Calvin down and pulled a flat, wide catalpa leaf off the tree. He scooped up the baby bird with it. Then he carried it to the garbage can. "Calvin, it's natural for dogs to hunt. That's what they do." Grandpa swept Calvin into his arms again.

Calvin clung to Grandpa.

"You'd better get some clothes on." Grandpa put Calvin down. Calvin ran inside.

Mikey looked over at the garbage can with the baby bird in it. Then he walked inside and sat down at the table. He didn't feel like eating anymore. It seemed every time he turned around, someone or something was ruined or lost or dead. And it didn't matter what anyone did; bad things happened anyway. Mikey looked at Calvin. Calvin's tears were gone now, but his face wore the same sadness Mikey felt.

By this time the kitchen was full. Julie sat in a high chair, slurping. Victoria stared sleepily at her empty bowl. Grandma stood in front of the table and held her hand over her Adam's apple. She liked to warm up her throat before singing her scales. She wore a happy, satisfied look. She didn't know the baby bird had died. "Put some clothes on, Calvin, and I'll get your bowl ready." Grandma hummed and added a bowl and spoon to the table.

Mamma looked in from the living room. "You

mean you're still not dressed? Here, Calvin, I'll get your suit."

Mamma came back holding Calvin's blue bathing suit.

"Oh, you saved my old bathing suit," said Calvin.

Mamma looked confused. "What are you talking about?"

Calvin slipped on his bathing suit and sat down at his bowl. "Yippy killed a baby bird."

"That's dreadful!" said Victoria.

Mamma shook her head. "Oh, dear."

"Its brothers will never know where it went," said Mikey.

Grandma walked around the table and put her hand on Mikey's head. She smoothed his hair.

"Grandpa put it in the garbage can. I hit Yippy, but Grandpa said she was supposed to do it." Calvin took a big mouthful of Cheerios. "Dogs hunt."

"Grandpa's right." Victoria nodded. "But it's still sad. We're going to have to protect the rest of those baby birds."

"How can a puppy be so mean?" said Mikey.

"Yippy didn't do it to be mean." Victoria yawned

and finally filled her cereal bowl. "It's her instinct."

"What's instinct?" asked Calvin.

"It's something you're born with. A feeling that makes you do something." Victoria drank her orange juice. "Yippy is just a baby dog, but she has an instinct that makes her hunt."

"Baby dog," said Julie. She banged her spoon on the tray of the high chair.

Mamma sighed. "I'm sorry this happened. I'll put Yippy on a shorter rope." She pressed her fingers to her lips in thought.

"You could move her to the front yard," said Mikey.

"Yes, that's it. I'll do it after the lessons. Okay, kids. When you finish, get on your suits." Mamma went back to the living room. "It's nine already," she called over her shoulder. "We have to hurry."

They finished their cereal quickly. Mikey went into the bedroom and opened his drawer. He was going swimming. There was no way out. He would plunge into the water the way that baby bird had plunged into the air. He looked at his skinny arms, sticking out of his pajama top like featherless wings. He wondered if there was ever a baby bird that was afraid to fly. And even if a baby bird wasn't, how did it know when it was ready to fly? How did it know when it spread its wings the first time that it wouldn't just jump to its death? Maybe that happened to some baby birds. Unlucky birds.

Mikey stared down at the contents of the drawer. Three neat stacks of clothes stared back at him. He looked through each one. No bathing suit. No, that couldn't be. It was just wishful thinking. He looked through a second time, carefully. He couldn't find it. A small smile crossed Mikey's face. He rifled through, throwing his clothes any which way. It was true: His suit was not there. Mikey whispered, "Thank you, God. Oh, thank you, thank you." He pushed his drawer closed.

Mikey went into the living room and sat in Grandpa's chair. He carefully kept the joy and excitement out of his voice. "Mamma, my bathing suit is gone." He reached for the remote control to the TV.

"What?" Mamma took the remote control from Mikey's hands and put it back on top of the TV. "I'll find it for you." She went back into the bedroom, with Mikey following. She opened his drawer and refolded the clothes as she searched for the suit.

Calvin came in. "What are you looking for in my drawer?"

"That's my drawer," said Mikey, "and don't you ever open it."

"It's mine," said Calvin. "See." He pointed to the drawers and counted, "One, two, three."

"Oh, Calvin, I'm sorry." Mamma pulled Calvin to her. "I confused you. I meant the third drawer from the top." She counted, pointing down from the top. "One, two, three."

"Oh," said Calvin in a flat tone. He pointed at the four pillows in a line on the double mattress on the floor. "Which is the third pillow?"

"That depends on which end you start counting from." Mamma knelt down and held Calvin by the shoulders. "You were right. You went to the third drawer. But you started at a different end from the one I had in mind."

"Oh." Calvin's face looked slightly less worried.

"Calvin," said Mamma, "did you take anything out of Mikey's drawer? Do you know where his bathing suit is?"

Suddenly Calvin smiled. "Oh! I thought you had

passed down Mikey's old bathing suit to me. So I took it."

"Where is it?" asked Mamma.

"Yippy ripped it up when I hit her with it."

"Oh no." Mamma got up and went outside. Mikey followed in his pajamas.

"Well, it's completely ruined." Mamma rolled the remains of the bathing suit into a tight ball.

"I guess I can't go swimming," said Mikey. "But that's okay. I understand."

"Oh no you don't, young man." Mamma bit her thumbnail. "You'll wear shorts. That's it. And this afternoon we'll get you another bathing suit."

"What?" Mikey's voice rose in horror. "I'll be the only nine-year-old in the beginner class—and besides that, I'll have to wear shorts!"

"Can you think of a better solution?"

"Calvin can wear shorts, and I'll wear his suit. It was his fault!"

"You can't fit in his suit."

"I'll miss the lesson today. They probably won't even do anything. They never do anything on the first day of lessons."

"No, that would be starting out on the wrong foot."

"And starting out in shorts isn't on the wrong foot?"

"It's better than not starting at all."

"Calvin and Julie and Victoria—all of them, every single one of them—ruin every bit of fun I have. They ruin my life!"

"Don't get dramatic, Mikey. And don't blame your problems on other people." Mamma went into the kitchen, calling over her shoulder, "Get your shorts on."

Mikey looked around wildly. He picked up a stick and threw it down hard. Yippy took the stick in her teeth and raced around the catalpa tree till she fell, tangled in the rope.

Calvin leaned out the window as they turned into the parking lot. "Is that the pool?"

"No, it's a mud puddle, cheese face," said Mikey.

"Of course it's the pool." Victoria patted the folded towel in her lap. "We're going to have fun."

They walked up to the office, following Mamma

in single file. Mikey felt as if they were a line of ducklings. "Quack," he said.

Mamma looked at Mikey strangely. Then her mouth opened in a circle of disappointment. "Ohh." She pointed to the sign beside the pool office. The sign was titled POOL RULES.

Rule 1. No unattended swimming
Rule 2. No horseplay or running
Rule 3. No street clothes in the pool

Mikey didn't bother to read the rest of the sign. He grinned. "Quack quack."

"All right, children." Mamma stood up tall and sighed loudly. "I'm going to have to go and buy Mikey a suit."

"Why don't I just skip today's lesson?"

"I'll only take a minute." Mamma took Julie by one hand and Calvin by the other. "Victoria and Mikey, if I don't get back in time, you'll have to check in at the office yourselves. And Mikey, don't quack."

"I want a green suit. Exactly like my last one," Mikey called at his mother's retreating back.

"I'll do the best I can."

"Let's sit down at the round table over here." Victoria led Mikey to a white metal table.

Mikey sat down and looked the place over. Beyond the fence was a large wading pool. On his side of the fence was a deep pool formed in an enormous L shape. At the bottom end of the L were three diving boards, two low ones and a higher one in the middle. Across from the diving boards at that end was a sliding board.

On the long part of the L there were no diving boards. But there was another slide. It was green and yellow plastic, and it curved. Mikey knew the colors were intended to make you feel happy. Kids were supposed to laugh and have a great time with that slide. He hated that slide.

There were numbers painted on the ground beside the pool. They started at two and went up to fourteen. "The numbers show how deep it is, huh?" he said casually.

Victoria pulled her eyes away from the group of girls over to their left and looked at the numbers. "The shallow end is only two feet deep."

"How tall am I?"

Victoria looked Mikey up and down. "I'm about four foot ten. And you're shorter than me. You must be about three foot ten."

"You're crazy. I'm not a whole foot shorter than you."

Victoria seemed to lose interest. She looked at the girls again. "You're taller than two feet. That's all that matters."

The water in the pool was clear. The top rippled as the wind blew across it. Mikey wondered if the water was cold. He hated cold water. He walked over to the edge of the pool, squatted, and dipped in his hand.

"Hey, kid!" A man in a white bathing suit came up to Mikey. "No swimming till the lessons begin." He was tan and hairy, like a monkey.

Mikey looked all the way up to his face and squinted into the sun. Then he stood and took a step away from the pool. The monkey-man went back into the office.

"Come sit down," said Victoria. "How's the water?"

"It's kind of cool."

"It's refreshing when it's cool."

Children were arriving steadily. They huddled around their mothers at the pool office. Mikey didn't recognize anyone from last summer. The Dumb Dunker was nowhere around. Mikey listened as the program director told the mothers which classes their children were in. A boy Mikey's size was in one of the beginner classes. Tracy was his teacher. A girl taller than Mikey was also in Tracy's class. Mikey perked up. The kids in Tracy's class were probably his age. He prayed he'd be in Tracy's class.

Mamma ran up, out of breath. "Here, Mikey. Run. There's a locker room in there. Bring me back your underwear and shorts."

"Quack." Mikey took the bag and went through the doorway with MEN printed over it. It was dark inside, and the floor was wet. Boys in various stages of undress stood everywhere. Mikey opened the bag. The bathing suit was green, but it wasn't like his last suit. It wasn't tight at the legs. Instead, it was like shorts with white net underpants sewed inside. Mikey looked around. No one else had on a bathing suit like that. He didn't want to wear it, but what choice did he have?

He put on the suit and went out of the locker room.

The Dumb Dunker, in a red-and-white-striped suit, walked right past Mikey. He was much taller this year and nowhere near as fat. He joined a group by the diving boards. Victoria was over in that group, too. Mikey wondered if Victoria was strong enough to work her way out from under if the Dumb Dunker dunked her. Should he go warn her? After class. The Dumb Dunker wouldn't dare act up during the lesson.

"You're in Tom's class." Mamma came up beside Mikey and pointed. Tom was the hairy monkey-man.

Mikey walked over and joined the group around Tom. Maybe Tom was an idiot and wouldn't remember that Mikey had put his hand in the pool before class. Mikey looked longingly at the beginner class that had gathered around the teacher named Tracy. No one in Tom's class looked older than seven. That meant Mikey was the oldest in the class. Everyone always expected the oldest one to learn the fastest. Mikey slumped his shoulders and bent his knees slightly. That made him shorter. He tried to put a stupid six-year-old's look on his face. Maybe no one would realize he was nine.

"Okay, everybody," said the monkey-man, "my name's Tom. We're going to have a blast. Let's jump in the pool now."

Everybody jumped in. As he hit the water, Mikey's bathing suit blew up like a balloon. He flattened it with both hands. The water came up to his waist. It was positively cold. He gave a quick shiver.

"Now put your face in the water and blow bubbles like this." Tom demonstrated.

Mikey put his face in the water and blew bubbles. Most of the children in the class did the same. Two children did not—a little girl and a slightly bigger boy. Both had on green bathing suits. Mikey looked at his own green bathing suit. Maybe green was a bad color.

Tom didn't seem to notice that the green-bathing-suit wearers weren't blowing bubbles. He looked around and smiled. "Okay, everybody, out of the pool. Stand on the side in a row."

Everyone got out of the pool and stood on the side in a row.

"The first step in swimming is getting wet all over." Tom stood in the water and reached for the first child on the left end of the row. It was a girl in a blue suit with ruffles across the bottom. She had a long braid, almost as long as Victoria's, and her eyes were now intense with expectation. Tom lifted her under the arms and carried her over to where the water was four feet deep. Mikey felt his stomach muscles tighten with worry. Suddenly Tom threw the girl up into the air. She screamed with delight and fell splashing into the water. Tom grabbed her as she came up. He lifted her back onto the side of the pool and told her to sit there with her legs in the water. Mikey's stomach was now a rock of fear. His knees felt weak. Tom reached for the second child and repeated the performance.

Mikey watched with unblinking eyes that by now burned from dryness. He was fourth in line. As Tom put number two back in his spot, Mikey walked behind the boy next to him so that he was now fifth in line. Tom repeated the same procedure with number three. Mikey grew pale. His throat was so tight he could barely swallow. He moved down one more position in line. Now he was sixth. Number four cried as he came up from his splash. He was the boy in the green bathing suit. He kept crying as Tom put him back in his spot.

Mikey moved to the very end of the line. He was tenth now. His heart beat hard and loud and drowned out the noise of the other children. Tom threw each child into the pool, one after the other. Number five sat on the side, dripping now. Number six had sopping wet hair hanging in her eyes. Tom reached for number seven. Now only two people stood between Mikey and sure death.

Suddenly Mikey leaned over the pool. He splashed both arms. He splashed his face. He splashed his hair. He ran behind the group and sat at the beginning of the row, on the far side of number one. He folded his hands in his lap and stared at his knees. Let Tom be an idiot, he prayed. Please God, let Tom not notice.

As Tom finished with the last boy, he stepped back. "I guess that's all of us," he said with a grin. "Yup, look how wet you all are." He walked through the water toward Mikey as he talked. "Especially you. Boy, I must have done you so long ago I can't even remember it. I'll have to do you again." He grabbed Mikey under the arms and threw him.

Mikey opened his mouth to scream. Water came in. It filled his mouth and nose and ears. He squeezed his eyes shut and fought. His foot hit the bottom of the pool, but he couldn't manage to stand up. He thrashed in every direction. His lungs felt as if they were about to burst. Then Tom was lifting him out and setting him on the side. Mikey coughed. He wiped the water out of his eyes and looked at the row of children. He counted. Ten.

They were all still alive. Tom had thrown them in against their will. He was unfair and dangerous. Any one of them could have drowned. But they hadn't. That was the important thing. They had stared death in the face and survived. All ten of them. Mikey looked at Tom in rage and triumph.

8

The Farm

Mikey watched expectantly as the family bit into their sandwiches.

"There's olives in my tuna fish," said Calvin.

"It's a new recipe." Mikey nodded. "Olives are good."

"And carrots," said Victoria. She picked one out of her sandwich and dropped it on her plate as though it was something disgusting. "Chopped carrots. Yuck."

"Diced, not chopped," said Mikey quickly.

"It doesn't matter," said Victoria. "Who ever heard of carrots in a sandwich? The person who made this recipe was a madman."

Mikey sighed. "I made it."

Grandma swallowed a big bite of sandwich and smiled. "Orange is a delightful color to find in a sandwich. And it contrasts so nicely with the black olives."

Mamma nodded. "Carrots are good for the eyes, and they protect against cancer. This is a wonderful sandwich."

"Look." Calvin had opened his sandwich and put the three black olives inside it on the tips of the three middle fingers of his right hand. He smiled proudly and ate them off.

Julie ripped apart what remained of her sandwich, and chunks of tuna fell onto the floor. She grabbed the olives and adorned her fingers. "Pretty," she said.

Grandpa looked around with confusion on his face. He turned up the dial on his hearing aid and dug an olive out of his sandwich. He looked around thoughtfully, rolling the olive between his thumb and forefinger.

"Another successful experiment, Mikey," said Daddy, finishing off his last bite. "I enjoyed that. Now let's hurry. It's time for the farm. I'll do the dishes." He stood up and patted Grandpa on the shoulder. "Eat that olive, Dad."

Grandpa popped the olive into his mouth.

Daddy went to the sink and filled it with sudsy water. "Mikey, when you finish, run down to the basement and get me the book lying on the shelf with Grandma's mason jars. It says *yearbook* on it. I want to bring it to Ray's."

"Sure, Dad." Mikey gulped away the sandwich and cleared his spot. He hurried down the steps. The shelf with the jars was near a big metal sink. There was the yearbook. On the next shelf down was a silver cap gun in a blue leather holster. Mikey could hardly believe how beautiful it was. He tucked the yearbook under his arm and picked up the gun and holster. He went upstairs with his heart pounding.

Mikey laid the book on the kitchen table. He carried the gun and holster to his father. "Look at these, Dad."

"Well, what do you know? My old cap gun."

"I found it when I cleaned out your closet," called Grandma from the living room. "I brought it down to the basement and worked some neat's-foot oil into the holster. Looks almost the way it used to."

"It sure does. Boy, this brings back memories." Daddy rubbed the gun lovingly and slid it into the holster. "You want it, Mikey?"

"Yes!" Mikey strapped on the holster. He took the gun out. "Can I have caps?"

"I think I can pick up some of those, too," said Grandpa.

"Mikey, I hate guns," said Mamma. She stood in the doorway. "Promise me you won't point that gun at anyone."

"It's just a toy, Mamma."

"It's a toy that makes a game of killing. Promise."

"Sure, Mamma," said Mikey. He held the gun with a firm grip.

Daddy opened the screen door. "Let's get in the car." The children piled into the station wagon with Yippy.

Ray's farm was only a ten-minute ride outside town. When they drove up the long, dusty driveway from the road, Ray was waiting for them. "Hello, city kids." Ray's smile was huge. "Better keep that dog in the car. Want to see the pigs first?"

They all got out of the station wagon with nods

and smiles, leaving Yippy jumping around inside, barking and banging her nose against the windows.

"There are the sows." Ray pointed. "And those are the pigs." He waved his arm toward the fat brown and pink bodies.

"Sows are pigs," said Victoria.

"You're right," said Ray. "But the ones we keep for breeding are called sows, and the others that go to the butcher are called pigs. That's farm talk."

"What's a butcher?" asked Calvin.

"He's the person that makes the pigs into meat," said Ray. "He slaughters them so you can eat pork chops and bacon."

"What does *slaughter* mean?" asked Calvin.

"Kill," said Mikey.

Calvin shrieked, "Daddy, he's going to kill the pigs!" He clutched Daddy around the legs.

"That's what they do to pigs. That's why farms raise them: to supply meat for people." Daddy stroked Calvin's hair.

Victoria swallowed and put on a fresh smile. "How many do you have here?"

"Oh, three, maybe four hundred."

Mikey let out a whistle. "Wow."

"That's how farming is these days, kids. You're into something in a big way or you're not into it at all." Ray led them toward a cow pen. "Those are the fat cows."

"They sure are fat," said Mikey.

"Yup," said Ray. "But that's not why we call them fat cows. Even those small ones over there are fat cows. Fat cows are the ones we fatten up for steak." Ray looked back at Calvin, who clung still closer to Daddy. "Maybe we should go look around the barn. I'll show you some old tools." He took off with Julie right behind and Daddy and Calvin straggling after.

Mikey stared at a large brown-and-white fat cow that stared back at him. The cow mooed. Mikey held up his cap gun and pointed it between the cow's eyes. "Bang. You're steak."

"Daddy, Mikey pointed his gun at a cow," said Victoria.

Daddy turned around. "Mikey, your mother told you not to point the gun at anyone."

"A cow isn't anyone," said Mikey. "Anyone is a person."

By now Ray and Julie had disappeared into the

barn. Calvin raced after them. Daddy gave Mikey a quick nod and hurried on to catch up with the others.

"A cow is alive," Victoria said to Mikey, "and you know Mamma meant not to point it at anything alive. Why do you need all those weapons anyway?"

"Weapons?"

Victoria counted off on her fingers: "The slingshot, the knife, the gun. Even your paper model tank. They're all weapons. It's an arsenal."

Mikey turned the gun over in his hands. Victoria's words made it seem as if he had done something wrong, but he didn't see what. He spoke slowly. "With a gun in my hands I feel ready."

"You see danger everywhere." Victoria snorted. "Even in an ordinary pool surrounded by people."

"Ordinary pools are deep."

"Yeah, but you act as though they're full of monsters. I watched you today. You know, there's nothing that's going to get you and pull you down."

"You don't know. Wait till the Dumb Dunker gets you."

"The Dumb Dunker?" Victoria looked bewildered.

"The tall kid in your swimming class. The one with the red-and-white-striped bathing suit. He'll get you."

"Oh, Kurt?"

Kurt? The Dumb Dunker had a normal name like Kurt?

"You mean you're afraid of Kurt? He's so cute!" Victoria laughed. "What a scaredy-cat you are!"

Mikey's voice rose. "Want a bullet in the heart?"

"Don't you even think about it, or I'll tell Mamma. I'm going to tell Mamma about the cow anyway."

Mikey didn't want to imagine what would happen if Victoria told Mamma. He threw up his hands. "How about if I put the gun in my pocket? Would that satisfy you?"

"No. Give it to me. I'll keep it safe."

"Never!" Mikey clenched his teeth.

"Okay, then, put it in the car."

Mikey shook his head.

"The car," said Victoria.

"Frog butt." Mikey ran to the car, opened a door, and tossed the gun onto the seat. Yippy bounded out and ran off toward the cow pen.

Mikey ran into the barn. "Daddy, Yippy's with the cows!"

"That's no problem," said Ray. "The cows are used to dogs. I just hope she stays away from the pigs. They could get nasty if she barks at them."

Ray led everyone out of the barn, into the bright sunlight. Yippy wagged her way up to them. She was green and stinking.

"She's been rolling in cow pies!" said Daddy. "Stand back." Daddy ran to catch Yippy.

Yippy ran past Calvin. Calvin dived to grab her. As he fell onto her, Yippy yipped and wriggled away. Daddy ran after her. Calvin stood up. His shirt was green and stinking. He started to cry. Julie hugged him. Her cheek and shirt were green and stinking. She rubbed at the green with both hands. Her hands were green and stinking.

"Let's all head for the hose," said Ray. "Your daddy can catch the dog."

"What happened?" Mamma took the bag of wet clothes that Calvin handed her. He and Julie now wore bathing suits.

"It was Mikey's fault," said Victoria.

"What did you do, Mikey?"

"I didn't do anything. Yippy did. She rolled in cow pies, and then everyone else got dirty from her."

"But it never would have happened if you hadn't let her out of the car," said Victoria. "And then Daddy chased Yippy all over the farm, and he got in such a bad mood that he wouldn't let us stay to go swimming. And it was all Mikey's fault."

"I didn't do it on purpose." Mikey's voice broke. "I didn't do it on purpose." He sat down on the kitchen floor.

Daddy came in the door and scowled at Mikey.

Grandma spoke quietly from her chair. "How did it happen?"

"Mikey shot a cow with his gun—," began Victoria.

"That's enough." Daddy spoke up quickly. "It doesn't matter. We're all okay. Dogs love the smell of farms. Yippy probably just wanted to perfume up a bit." Daddy wrinkled his nose. "She did a good job."

"You all smell." Mamma wrinkled her nose, too.

"Go take a bath. We've been invited to some friends' house for dinner. And you can thank your dad that your suits are still dry—because all of you need to wear your bathing suits over there."

Mikey looked at his mother as the rest of the family trooped off. "They have a pool? Does everyone in the world have to have a pool or a watering hole or some other stupid place to drown?"

"It's a baby pool," said Mamma, "to wade in. Get up now, Mikey."

"No."

Mamma stood silent for a moment. Then she sat down on the floor beside Mikey.

Mikey looked at her waiting face. "Everything goes wrong."

"What a silly thing to say."

Mikey thought of his slingshot rubber bands lost down the heating vent, of his picture for Daddy that Calvin wrote on, of his ice cream that Julie fed to Yippy, of his precious knife that he'd never see again, of his awful new bathing suit that blew up like a balloon. There was no doubt about it: Mikey had rotten luck. Plus even things that weren't a matter of luck went wrong. "I can't do anything right, Mamma. Nothing."

"Why, Mikey, what on earth do you mean?"

"I can't swim. I can't draw. I can't whittle. I can't even keep the dog in the car."

"Whittle?"

"Yeah. But don't worry, I lost the knife."

"Oh." Mamma seemed to think about that.

"People get old and birds die, and all I do is open the car door and let the dog out and make a mess of everything."

Mamma put her arms around Mikey. "This is getting pretty complicated." She hugged him close. "You're doing fine, Mikey. You can't be responsible for everything that goes on. None of us can. It's hard enough being responsible for ourselves." She put her hand on his cheek. "You're doing really fine. You work hard at everything and you're a good person and I'm proud of you."

"I wish I could do just one thing really good, Mamma."

"You do lots of things really good, Mikey. You're the best in the family on a bike. You're a great cook.

And you're a terrific aim with a baseball or anything else." Mamma pulled Mikey onto her lap. "You know what I think? I think what's really getting you down is this swimming thing. Does that sound right to you?"

Mikey sighed. "Yes."

"You've always been cautious, Mikey. When you were little, you looked both ways about fifty times before you crossed the street. But you crossed, Mikey. You convinced yourself it was safe, and you crossed." Mamma put her chin on the top of Mikey's head. "I don't know how it happened. Maybe because Victoria teases you so much, your fear has compounded over the years. It's become some big thing with you. I wish I could help you."

Mikey swallowed the lump in his throat and nestled into his mother's arms. "I wish everything was good."

"Things are going to get better, Mikey."

"Promise?"

Mamma pulled herself back so that she could face Mikey. She closed her mouth tight and looked at him hard. "It's for you to promise yourself. If you have confidence and look at things positively, they will seem better. And you'll be happier. That I can promise."

Mikey looked at Mamma with hope.

"It's up to you, Mikey," she whispered. "Think positively."

Mikey kissed his mother's cheek and got up. "I'll try."

9

The Friends' Pool

"Everybody get in the car," said Daddy. "Hurry."

Victoria, Julie, and Mikey filed out the back door.

"Where's Calvin? Go get him, Mikey."

Mikey went into the bedroom. It was empty. He went into Grandma and Grandpa's bedroom. Calvin sat on the bed. He had on pink lipstick and several necklaces. His fingers dazzled with jewels.

"Hi, Mikey. Look at me."

"Boys don't wear lipstick and necklaces."

"I'm a boy, and I wear lipstick and necklaces."

Grandma came up behind Mikey. "What are you doing with my good jewelry?" She stood in the doorway, hesitating. "Calvin, please take those things off right now. And don't use my lipstick without asking me."

"It's mine." Calvin held the lipstick tight in his fist as Grandma took the jewelry off him. "Victoria gave it to me in the car as a treat. Can't I have just one necklace to wear?"

"This stuff isn't for boys," said Grandma. Her face was troubled.

Calvin watched Grandma put the jewelry away. His eyes filled with tears.

"You have to think positively," said Mikey suddenly in a loud, firm voice. "Boys can wear jewelry in the house. Sure, why not? They don't wear it outside with strangers and people, unless they're rock stars"—he looked right at Grandma—"or opera singers or something like that. But they wear it at home with family. Right, Calvin?"

Calvin stared at Mikey with a stupefied look. "Unnn, yeah."

"Can't he have a necklace to wear when he's in the house?"

Calvin jumped up. "Can't I?"

"Well," said Grandma slowly, "I suppose if rock stars and opera singers can do it . . ." She lifted her eyebrows quickly and nodded. "These are new times. Attitudes have changed." She opened the drawer and pulled out an old padded pink jewelry box. As she lifted the lid, it played music. "I'd forgotten about this stuff. It's old costume jewelry." She laughed. "I saved it for my own daughter, but I never had a daughter. Maybe all you children would like to play with it." She handed the box to Calvin. "How about this? Wear the jewelry anywhere you like. But please keep the lipstick for the house only."

Their car pulled up into the friends' driveway. Mikey could see the wading pool in the side yard. A toddler sat in the water. He had lots of short, curly hair. Two girls in bathing suits stood beside the pool. A wave of recognition splashed over Mikey. He smiled. They had played with these girls last summer. The smaller girl was just a year younger than Mikey. The bigger one was Victoria's age.

"Hi, Jessica." Victoria got out, grinning. "Hi, Catlain."

Calvin and Julie and Mikey got out of the car.

Jessica and Catlain ran up. "I remember you," said Catlain, smiling at Mikey.

"Look." Calvin opened a plastic bag and took out a string of beads.

"What a pretty necklace. Is it yours?" Catlain touched it lightly.

"Grandma gave it to me." Calvin looked at Mikey. "Just for Iowa," he added quickly. "Not for keeps."

"Put it on," said Catlain. She took Calvin by the hand. "Come see my mother and my baby brother. They're in the pool."

Catlain's mother sat beside the wading pool. Catlain's baby brother stood in the pool and poured water from a bucket onto a plastic boat. Calvin jumped into the wading pool and picked up a rubber alligator. Julie sat in the grass and held up a cricket. "See?" The two boys scrambled out of the pool, squealing, and ran to her.

"Let's go next door," said Catlain to Mikey. "They have a real pool there."

"I want to stay here," said Mikey.

"Okay." Catlain ran over to a lounge chair. Behind it was a basketful of water toys. She handed Mikey a red-and-white blow-up ball. "You blow up the ball, and I'll blow up the shark."

"Are you a good swimmer?" asked Mikey between puffs.

"I just learned."

"I'm taking lessons at the city pool," said Mikey.

"I took lessons there last month. That's how I learned." Catlain put the plug into the shark tube. "Want an apple?"

"Sure."

Catlain ran into the house. Mikey followed. She handed him an apple and grabbed one for herself.

Mikey walked over to the birdcage by the window. "I have a bird that looks just like yours, except mine has two feet."

Catlain laughed. "You're very funny."

"Huh?" said Mikey. At that moment the parakeet ruffled its feathers and shifted its weight. A second foot descended from under its belly. What a dumb thing to say! Mikey knew birds stood on one foot now and then. It was as though his mind had gone blank. Mikey smiled in embarrassment, but Catlain had already started for the door.

"Come on outside."

Mikey followed Catlain. The sun was warm on his

back. They sat at the picnic table and swung their legs as they ate.

"Want to go next door now?" Catlain put her apple core on the table.

"No. I want to go back to the wading pool. Maybe I'll play alligator with Calvin. You can go on if you want."

"I'll go to the wading pool, too."

Jessica and Victoria ran up to them. "Come into the big pool with us," said Jessica. "We're doing somersaults under the water."

"Okay, I'll come," said Catlain.

Mikey looked at them.

"Mikey, you better not come with us," said Victoria. She stood beside him and put her arm around his shoulder from behind. "You better stay with Calvin so he won't be sad and lonely."

"You're right," said Mikey. He wanted to hug Victoria for saving him like that, but the girls were already running off. Victoria had been nice to him. Somehow that made things seem worse. He was mad he had needed someone to be nice to him. Mad at himself. Mikey watched the girls turn the corner of the house. A sudden cold longing settled in his chest.

10

Swimming

Children arrived at the city pool in groups of two and three and four. They laughed and joked and ran to the spots where their teachers had told them to wait.

"Bye, Grandma. Thanks for driving us." Victoria went to the far corner of the fenced-in area, and another girl greeted her with a smile.

Mikey looked around. His group sat on the concrete near the end of the pool where they had their lesson. He was in no rush to join them. He stood quietly beside Grandma.

"Mikey," said Grandma, "it's still early. Want to sit with me a minute at that table?"

"Sure."

They went to a round metal table with a huge umbrella stuck in the middle.

Grandma put her hand over her throat and looked off. "Do you hate your lessons?" she asked.

"Oh, I don't know."

"Victoria said your teacher threw you into the water yesterday."

"She told you?"

"Yes." Grandma tapped her fingernail on her top teeth. Mikey wondered if she was testing for hollowness. Maybe she had a cavity. "That was a dreadful thing he did."

Mikey shrugged. "He's not so bad."

"He'd leave you alone if you didn't call attention to yourself."

Mikey thought of the day before—how he'd splashed himself with water and run to the front of the line. How much had Victoria told Grandma? How much had Victoria seen? Mikey looked away.

"What are you most afraid of, Mikey?"

Mikey was taken by surprise. "You mean, in swimming?"

"Yes."

Mikey was silent for a moment. Then he said softly, "Dying."

Grandma nodded wisely. "Well, there's your problem."

Mikey felt stupid. "What do you mean?"

"You can't think of it in dire terms like that—living or dying. Think of it in smaller terms. What moment are you most afraid of?"

"What moment?" repeated Mikey.

"Yes. What moment sets off that feeling of panic?"

"When the water closes over my head."

"Well now, see? That's all you're afraid of," said Grandma. "It's simple. All you have to do is get past that moment, and you'll be fine."

But if his head stayed underwater, he'd die. Mikey looked at Grandma suspiciously. Was she getting too old to understand that?

She smiled at him. "Doesn't that feel better?"

Mikey nodded doubtfully.

"Sometimes I'll be singing—you know, while I'm doing the laundry or something—and I won't notice that a neighbor's come into the house. And when I realize it, for an instant I'll be all flustered at the idea that someone heard me." Grandma folded her hands together and set them on the table. "Know what I do then?"

Mikey shook his head.

"I sing louder. I pretend I'm Maria Callas or Joan Sutherland. I belt it out." Grandma laughed.

Mikey laughed.

"Afterward I always treat myself to a banana split." She pinched Mikey's arm and smiled mischievously. "And I don't even really like banana splits anymore. Too rich."

Mikey laughed again.

"Do you like banana splits?"

"Yes."

"Well, today after the lesson, if you get past the moment when the water closes over your head without panicking, then just tell me it's banana split time, and I'll take everyone to Birdsall's ice-cream parlor."

Tom came out of the pool office and walked toward Mikey's group. Mikey felt a quick rush of anger as the memory of the first lesson came back. But he had survived yesterday. He would survive today, too. Mikey stood up. "That's my teacher. I've got to go."

"Your mom's bringing Julie and Calvin to the wading pool later, so she'll take you home." Grandma got up. "Remember, Mikey, today you pretend. How about those young swimmers we saw in the Olympics last year? Now those were fine swimmers. You can be a medal winner." She gave a smile and a wave and left.

Mikey thought about Grandma's words. He should pretend. Just jump in and pretend he could swim. But what if he sank? Well, he should pretend he couldn't sink. He should pretend something was holding him up. Mikey remembered how his new bathing suit had blown up like a balloon when he first jumped into the water. That was it. He could pretend his suit was holding him up.

How far could pretending take him?

"Hi, kids," said Tom. "When I blow my whistle, jump in the water and get wet all over. And I mean all over." He looked across the group of children. His eyes settled on Mikey. "And if you get scared, just put your arms up. You'll always get to the top of the water if your arms are above your head." He blew the whistle. The children jumped in. The girl in the blue bathing suit with the ruffles on the bottom sat down on the floor of the pool. Her hair was loose today, and it was so long the tips of it floated on the surface of the water above her. She came up and spit water. She looked at Mikey expectantly.

Mikey looked back at the girl with steady eyes. He was certain that if he didn't get wet all over, Tom would throw him in—and he never wanted Tom to throw him in again. "I have a secret balloon," he said to the girl. Mikey sank to the floor of the pool. He came up coughing and choking—and alive.

The girl nodded slowly. "A secret balloon," she whispered.

"We're going to work on floating and kicking today," said Tom. "First, everyone hold on to the sides, and kick your legs out behind you, like this."

The children all held on to the sides and kicked. Mikey kicked as hard as he could. He put every positive thought he had into kicking and kicking and kicking.

"A powerful kick is a kick from a pair of straight legs. If you bend your knees, you don't go anywhere."

Mikey made his knees straight and hard as stone.

"It's time to float," said Tom. "Lie facedown in

the water with your arms over your head. That's the dead man's float."

Lousy name, thought Mikey. The children watched Tom float. It seemed forever. Maybe he was really dead. But his head popped up, and he let out a puff of air. "Now you do it. Keep those arms out straight above your head."

The girl in the blue bathing suit nudged Mikey. She smiled. "Me first." She lay on her stomach in the water and floated.

"I have a secret balloon," Mikey said to the girl, even though she couldn't hear him with her face in the water. "I can't drown today." He closed his eyes and lay facedown in the water with his arms over his head. He felt himself sink. The water closed over his body and head. This was it. If he could just get past this moment. . . . He felt himself rise again. The back of his head broke the surface of the water. His bottom was in the air. His bathing suit was working! Mikey stood up and looked around.

"Good, kid," Tom said to Mikey. "Do it again."

Mikey looked at the girl in the blue bathing suit. She nodded and did another dead man's float. Mikey did another dead man's float.

"Try putting your kick together with your float," said Tom.

Mikey did it. He practiced his floating and kicking around the end of the pool. The girl in the blue bathing suit joined him. Another boy held on to the side near them and kicked. Pretty soon the boy let go, and all three of them floated and kicked.

Tom sloshed through the water over to them. "Move your arms like this to pull you through the water." He did the stroke Victoria had taught Mikey. "That's the freestyle. The crawl."

"I know," said Mikey.

They did it.

"We'll work on your breathing later. For now keep those arms moving. High elbows when you bring them out of the water." Tom went back to work with the children who were still practicing their kicks. Mikey and the girl in the blue bathing suit and the other boy all circled their arms like windmills and kicked and floated. The whistle for the end of the lesson blew. Tom turned to the three children. "That's called swimming, kids." Then he pointed at

Mikey. "You're a fast learner. I didn't think you had it in you yesterday."

Children climbed out of every side of the pool. Some ran to the lockers. Others laughed and chased each other.

Mikey stood in the water and repeated Tom's words. They were wonderful words. Fabulous words.

"It's not really swimming."

Mikey jumped around.

The voice came from the big boy in Tracy's beginner class. "My sister told me. I've been doing that floating stuff for a month. It's not swimming till you can do it in deep water."

"Oh." Mikey hated to admit it, but the boy sounded right.

The boy splashed Mikey as he went past.

"He's not very nice."

Mikey jumped again.

This time the voice was from the little girl in the blue bathing suit. "I think we swam."

"But probably we couldn't do it in deep water." Mikey imagined trying to float in deep water. What would it be like to have the water close over his head, knowing that if he put his feet down, the bottom would be out of range? He gave an involuntary jerk of the shoulders. "At least I couldn't."

"I could." The little girl got out of the pool. "If you have a secret balloon, I do too." She ran over to the ladder at the five-foot mark and climbed down to the third rung. "Watch." She flung herself into the water, twisting as she did it, so that she splashed in facedown.

Mikey got out of the pool in a panic. He watched the little girl's hair go all the way under the water. He felt the same cold fear he'd felt when Calvin had slipped under the water in the motel pool. All the noises were fading away. His arms and legs were heavy, like lead. But he couldn't let himself freeze up. He had to fight it. The little girl might need him. She didn't have a balloon. And suddenly he was running to the ladder. He could see the girl way down near the bottom. She spun around and grabbed hold of the ladder. She was pulling herself up. But she stopped. She doubled over. Bubbles came from her mouth. She was in trouble! Maybe her hair was caught in the ladder!

"Help!" Mikey shouted. No one seemed to notice. "Help!" He looked for a life preserver. There wasn't one. He climbed down the ladder, using it to pull himself under the water. As long as he held on to the ladder, he wouldn't die. He could keep himself safe and he could help the little girl. Daddy had said so. As long as he held on to the ladder, they'd both be fine.

The little girl grabbed Mikey around the legs. She was stronger than he'd expected. He had to turn himself upside down to get past her arms to her hair. He yanked at it.

But her hair didn't seem to be caught in anything. Mikey pushed her upward. She kicked out. Her foot caught him on the shoulder, knocking him away from the ladder and to the bottom of the pool. Suddenly she moved upward as though jet-propelled. And she was gone.

Mikey sank to the bottom, his hands clutching at the water. He looked around. He was alone on the floor of the pool. He could see the ladder, but he couldn't reach it. His blood hummed in his ears. Yet over that hum Tom's words resounded: "You'll always get to the top of the water if your arms are

above your head." Mikey put his arms straight out over his head with his hands together, just like in the dead man's float. Now was the moment for his balloon bathing suit to work. *Come on, suit.* His chest started to hurt. *Please, suit, come on!* And now he was rising, slowly. He kicked with straight legs. His hands broke through the surface of the water. His head came bursting up, and he gasped for air. A hand caught his and pulled him to the ladder. He climbed out.

"You okay, kid?" Tom slapped Mikey between the shoulder blades.

Mikey looked at the little girl in the blue bathing suit. She was pale and shivering. But she was okay. And so was Mikey, so was Mikey. Relief spread across his chest and down his body. It was good to be alive. He nodded.

"That was a bad idea. Never go in after someone unless you know lifesaving techniques."

"Yeah."

"You hear me? You could have drowned."

"I won't do it again."

"Good." Tom took the little girl in the blue suit by the hand. "Is that cramp gone? Let's go get a towel and wrap you up." He turned to Mikey. "You came up by yourself, you know. I pulled Emma up. But you came up by yourself."

Mikey listened to Tom's words. His heart beat hard and fast. He felt warm all over. "Yeah, I did," he almost shouted.

"You did okay, kid." Tom and Emma walked away.

"Bye, Emma," called Mikey.

Emma rubbed at her temple. "You pulled my hair." Then she smiled. "Sort of like a caveman. Bye."

Mikey ran around the pool and past the crowds of new children waiting for the next set of lessons. He ran all the way into the wading pool area. All the way to his mother. "I can swim! I can swim, Mamma! Want to see?" Mikey hopped into the wading pool and did a crawl stroke with his arms and the flutter kick with his legs.

"That's terrific, Mikey," said Mamma, crying.

"Then why are you crying?"

"Because I'm so happy for you."

"I can't swim," said Calvin.

Mamma put her arm around Calvin. "Your time will come," she said. "Today is Mikey's day."

Mikey came out of the pool. He ran up to Julie, who was dancing on tiptoe on the concrete. "Kiss me, twinkle toes. I can swim."

Julie threw her arms around Mikey and kissed him on the lips. Mikey hugged her tight.

Victoria came up. "My lesson got out late," she said to Mamma. She turned to Mikey. "Daddy said you could have your gun back after swimming class. Maybe if you're nice to me, we can pretend we're on a hunt."

"Okay. But right now there's something better than my gun." Mikey grinned. "Right now I don't even care about guns. I don't care about slingshots. I don't care about knives." He laughed. "I can swim! I can swim, Victoria." He ran in a circle around her.

Victoria laughed happily. "Really?"

"This bathing suit saved me. It's my secret balloon." Mikey plunged in and did his kick-float.

"That's wonderful," said Victoria. "But, Mikey, it's not your bathing suit. Be logical. Bathing suits don't save people."

Mikey thought about that. Was it true? He looked down at his bathing suit. It seemed ordinary in every way. He looked at Victoria—his sister who always knew everything, who always felt confident. Maybe she was right. She had to be. But for a while Mikey would always wear this exact bathing suit when he went in deep water. He smiled at Victoria and gave a silent nod.

Grandma came walking through the entrance to the pool area. "Hello, everyone."

"Hi," said Mamma. "I didn't expect to see you here. Did you forget I was picking up the kids?"

"No. I just had to ask Mikey a question." She turned to Mikey and looked at him steadily. "I was wondering, Mikey, could you tell me what time it is?"

Mamma and Victoria looked from Grandma to Mikey blankly.

Mikey stood tall. "Banana split time."

Calvin jumped in place. "I love banana splits."

"Are we going out for banana splits?" asked Victoria.

"How perfect," said Mamma. "Mikey has something to celebrate."

"I know," said Grandma.

"Banana banana," said Julie.

Mikey smiled.

About the Author

Donna Jo Napoli teaches linguistics and is the author of several children's novels. She lives in Swarthmore, Pennsylvania, with her family.